Sesame Street Start-to-Read Books™
help young children take a giant step into reading.
The stories have been skillfully written, designed,
and illustrated to provide funny, satisfying
reading experiences for the child just starting out.
Let Big Bird, Bert and Ernie, Oscar the Grouch,
and all the Sesame Street Muppets get your child
into reading early with these wonderful stories!

LEIGH

On *Sesame Street,* Susan is played by Loretta Long, Bob by Bob McGrath, Mr. McIntosh by Chet O'Brien, and Gordon by Roscoe Orman.

Library of Congress Cataloging-in-Publication Data:

Hautzig, Deborah. It's not fair! (A Sesame Street start-to-read book) SUMMARY: When irresponsible Ernie seems to be taking all the credit for Bert's hard work on their lemonade stand, it provokes an angry outburst from Bert and threatens their friendship. [1. Anger—Fiction. 2. Friendship—Fiction. 3. Puppets—Fiction] I. Leigh, Tom, ill. II. Henson, Jim. III. Children's Television Workshop. IV. Sesame Street (Television program) V. Title. VI. Series: Sesame Street start-to-read books. PZ7.H2888It 1986 [E] 85-30154 ISBN: 0-394-88151-6 (trade); 0-394-98151-0 (lib. bdg.)

Manufactured in the United States of America 1 2 3 4 5 6 7 8 9 0

It's Not Fair!

by Deborah Hautzig • illustrated by Tom Leigh

Featuring Jim Henson's Sesame Street Muppets

Random House/Children's Television Workshop

One hot summer day
Ernie had a cool idea.
"Hey, Bert," he said.
"Let's sell lemonade."

"Good idea, Ernie,"
said Bert.
"You go buy the lemons.
Then we will make
the lemonade together."

"Right, Bert," said Ernie.

"I will get the lemons."

And he ran off to the store.

On the way Ernie saw
Big Bird and Grover.
"Hi," said Ernie.
"I am going to have
a lemonade stand.
Be sure to come."

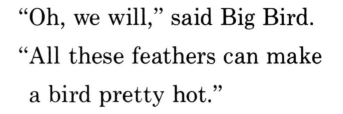

"Oh, we will," said Big Bird.
"All these feathers can make
a bird pretty hot."

At Mr. McIntosh's store Ernie saw
big piles of lemons.
He saw big piles of oranges too.
The oranges looked delicious.
Ernie bought them
instead of lemons.

At Ernie and Bert's house
Bert painted letters
on a piece of cardboard.
They said:

ICE-COLD LEMONADE

10¢ A GLASS

When Ernie got home,
Bert looked inside the bag.
"ERNIE! These are oranges!"
he yelled.
"Where are the lemons?"

"At the store," said Ernie.

Bert groaned.

"We need LEMONS for lemonade!

I will get the lemons.

And you finish painting the sign,"

said Bert.

Ernie said, "Sure, Bert."

Bert went to the store.
Susan and Bob were there.
Bert told everyone
what had happened.
They all laughed.

"You know how Ernie is.
We can't expect him
to get it right,"
said Susan.
"Lucky he has Bert," said Bob.
"Lucky?" said Bert to himself.
"It is not very lucky for ME!"

Bert came home to a kitchen
covered with blue paint.
Ernie was covered with paint too.
"ERNIE! What a mess you made,"
said Bert.
"Now I have to clean up
and YOU have to take a bath."

"Right, Bert," said Ernie.

"You start making the lemonade.

I will not be long."

Bert squeezed the lemons.

He added sugar and ice water.
He filled a big pitcher
with lemonade.

Then he made the sign
look nice and neat.

At last Ernie came back.

He was sprinkling powder

on himself.

Most of it fell on the floor.

"Hi, Bert! I am ready to help now."

"HELP?" yelled Bert.

"You are no help at all!"

Bert set up the lemonade stand.
Grover and Big Bird were
the first to come.
"Mmmm. This lemonade
is terrific, Ernie," said Grover.
Big Bird said, "It sure is.
"Ernie always has good ideas."

Bert glared at Ernie.
"It is easy to have ideas,"
Bert grumbled to himself.
"It is not so easy
to make them work."

Susan and Bob came.

So did Gordon and Mr. McIntosh.

Everyone was thirsty.

Clink, clink went their dimes.

"Ernie got the lemons at my store,"
Mr. McIntosh told everyone proudly.
"Lemons?" grumbled Bert.
"Ernie got ORANGES.
I got the lemons."

Gordon patted Ernie on the back.
"You did a great job," he said.
Ernie smiled. "Thanks, Gordon.
Maybe I will do this every day!"

Bert got red in the face.

"EVERY DAY?" he said.

"Sure, Bert!" said Ernie.

"I will call it

Ernie's Famous Lemonade!"

Bert could not

stand it anymore.

"IT'S NOT FAIR!"
Bert shouted.
"I did all the work.
I ALWAYS do all the work.
Ernie makes a mess.
Ernie makes mistakes.
But he has all the fun.
And everybody expects me
to do everything."

Then Bert burst into tears.

"Nobody ever even says thank you,"
he said, and ran inside.

"Oh, this is so SAD!"
said Grover. He blew his nose.

"Gee," said Big Bird.

"I never knew Bert could cry."

Bob said, "Everybody can cry."

"Especially when everyone
forgets about them,"
said Susan.
Everyone felt terrible.

Ernie felt the worst of all.
"I have to show Bert
that I am really sorry.
I will give him a present,"
he said.
He left to look for
the perfect surprise for Bert.

When Ernie got home,

he peeked into the kitchen.

Bert was sniffling sadly.

"I am sorry, Bert," said Ernie.

"I got you a present

to cheer you up.

Please don't cry anymore!"

Ernie gave Bert the present.

Bert stopped sniffling.

He opened the present.

His frown turned into a smile.

"Oh, Ernie! How wonderful!

A dustpan and brush!" said Bert.

"But you spent all

the lemonade money on me."

Ernie smiled shyly.

"That is okay," he said.

"You did all the work."

Bert could not wait to try out
the new dustpan and brush.
He began sweeping up the powder.
"I will help, old buddy,"
said Ernie.

"No," said Bert.

"I LIKE to sweep.

Anyway, I sweep

better than you!

But you can

keep me company, old pal."

And Ernie did.